Run! Run! It's Scary Poo!

Susan Gates & Charles Fuge

PUFFIN

To Laura, Alex and Chris
S.G.

For Sarah Churchill (shrew expert)
C.F.

PUFFIN BOOKS
Published by the Penguin Group
Penguin Books Ltd, 80 Strand, London WC2R 0RL, England
Penguin Group (USA), Inc., 375 Hudson Street, New York, New York 10014, USA
Penguin Books Australia Ltd, 250 Camberwell Road, Camberwell, Victoria 3124, Australia
Penguin Books Canada Ltd, 10 Alcorn Avenue, Toronto, Ontario, Canada M4V 3B2
Penguin Books India (P) Ltd, 11 Community Centre, Panchsheel Park, New Delhi – 110 017, India
Penguin Group (NZ), cnr Airborne and Rosedale Roads, Albany, Auckland 1310, New Zealand
Penguin Books (South Africa) (Pty) Ltd, 24 Sturdee Avenue, Rosebank 2196, South Africa

Penguin Books Ltd, Registered Offices: 80 Strand, London WC2R 0RL, England

www.penguin.com

First published 2004
1 3 5 7 9 10 8 6 4 2

Text copyright © Susan Gates, 2004
Illustrations copyright © Charles Fuge, 2004

The moral right of the author and illustrator has been asserted

Set in Myriad Tilt

Manufactured in China

British Library Cataloguing in Publication Data
A CIP catalogue record for this book is available from the British Library

ISBN 0–141–38006–3

Tiny Shrew stared up at the jungle trees.
It was his first time outside his cosy nest.
He had a **lot** to learn.

"Right," said Ma Shrew.
"Let's get cracking! You need
to know how to tell safe
poo from scary poo."

"Pardon?" asked Tiny Shrew, puzzled.
"We shrews can't *see* danger," said Ma Shrew, blinking her poor,
weak eyes. "But we can *smell* it. We just have to sniff some poo
and we can tell if it's parrot poo. Or ... PANTHER POO!"

Tiny Shrew shuddered, he'd heard about panthers.

They were terrible creatures. They were black as night.

They had deep, low growls. **Grrrrr!**

They padded about on almost silent paws.

And they liked to snack on shrews.

"What do we do if it's panther poo?" asked Tiny Shrew.

"Run like mad!" said Ma Shrew.

They went into the jungle to practise. Tiny Shrew bumped into something.
His long, shrewy nose got busy. **Sniff! Sniff!**
Could it possibly be…?

"It's scary poo!
Run, Ma! Run for your life!"

But Ma Shrew didn't run.
She just stood there,
tapping her toes.

"Calm down," she
told Tiny Shrew.
"That's not scary poo."
"Is it safe poo, then?" asked Tiny Shrew.
"It's not poo at all!" said Ma Shrew with a
big sigh. "It's a butterfly."

Ma Shrew told Tiny Shrew to try again. "Sniff this!" she said.

Tiny Shrew crinkled his long, shrewy nose. He took a little sniff.

Then he took a big, deep sniff and… "Aaaaargh!

Run, Ma. Run for your life!" he screamed. "It's scary panther poo!"

Then he hid behind a rock, hoping the panther wouldn't see him.

But Ma stayed exactly where she was. "That wasn't scary poo either," she said.

"Oh," said Tiny Shrew. "So was it safe poo?"

"No," said Ma Shrew. "You just sniffed a bird."

The next day, Ma Shrew took Tiny Shrew out for another lesson. "Right. Forget about yesterday," she said. "Sniff this."
Tiny Shrew took a **long**, deep sniff...

"Aaaaargh! It's poo!
It's scary panther poo. Run for your life!"

"No, no, **no!** That wasn't a panther you sniffed," cried Ma Shrew. "That was a toad."
Tiny Shrew went pink with shame.

Ma Shrew told Pa Shrew what had happened.
"This is serious," she said. "I've tried all sorts,
but he just can't smell scary poo."
"But how can he survive in the jungle if he can't
sniff out danger?" said Pa Shrew, sounding worried.
Tiny Shrew heard his parents talking.
"I'm not going outside tomorrow," he thought.
"I'm staying down here. Where it's safe."

So the next day, when Big Brother said,
"Why don't you come out to play?"
Tiny Shrew said, "No way!"
  "Na, na, na, na, na!" teased Big Brother.
"You can't sniff out anything – you're
going to be panther lunch!"
  So Tiny Shrew sat in his dark den,
feeling very miserable.

He heard all the little shrews playing, up
in the sunshine. He heard their shouts of
laughter. But when he listened hard...
he heard something else too.

He heard a soft, low snarl…

Rrrrrr

And an even quieter sound…

Pad…
    Pad…
Pad…
    Pad…

Creeping closer to the shrew children,
on *almost silent paws* was a PANTHER!
Tiny Shrew didn't stop to think.
He dashed out of his den…

... straight into something black and bristly.

WHUMP!

He bit it as hard as he could.

CHOMP!

"Grrrrrrr!"

An angry growl made the jungle
leaves shiver. All shrew children
knew that sound...

... PANTHER!

As the shrew children scattered, Tiny Shrew
clung on tight to the panther's tail with his
teeth. But the panther lashed his tail and
Tiny Shrew couldn't hold on any longer...

Tiny Shrew flew through the air and landed with
a **plop** in something soft and squishy.
"I'm stuck!" he cried, as he
tried to struggle free.

Of course, Tiny Shrew couldn't smell what he'd landed in, but Ma and Pa could.
They came racing to the rescue and tugged out Tiny Shrew.
"Run!" yelled Ma. "Run for your life!
It's scary panther poo…"

"Don't panic," said Tiny Shrew, "the panther's miles away now."
"What do you mean?" asked Pa.

Big Brother came running back. "It's true," he said.
"Tiny Shrew scared off the panther. He's a hero!"
All the shrew children cheered.
Tiny Shrew went pink with pride.

"But how did you sniff out the panther?" asked Pa.
"I didn't!" said Tiny Shrew. "I didn't smell him.
I *heard* him! I can hear even the tiniest sounds."
"Then you'll be safe in the jungle after all!"
Pa said, sounding relieved.

Ma Shrew gave Tiny Shrew a **big** hug – then she wished she hadn't!
"Come on, you hero," she said, "let's go home and get cleaned up."